D0131043

FOR ATLAS

Copyright © 2019 by Jonty Howley

All rights reserved. Published in the United States by Random House Children's Books,
a division of Penguin Random House LLC, New York.

Random House and the colophon are registered trademarks of Penguin Random House LLC.

Visit us on the Web!
rhcbooks.com

Educators and librarians, for a variety of teaching tools, visit us at RHTeachersLibrarians.com

Library of Congress Cataloging-in-Publication Data
Names: Howley, Jonty, author, illustrator.
Title: Big boys cry / Jonty Howley.
Description: New York : Random House, [2019] | Summary: As he walks to his new school,
a frightened Levi learns that it is okay for big boys to cry.
Identifiers: LCCN 2018030323 (print) | LCCN 2018035911 (ebook) |
ISBN 978-1-5247-7320-5 (hardcover) | ISBN 978-1-5247-7321-2 (hardcover library binding) |
ISBN 978-1-5247-7322-9 (ebook)
Subjects: | CYAC: Crying—Fiction. | Fathers and sons—Fiction. | First day of school—Fiction.
Classification: LCC PZ7.1.H689 (ebook) | LCC PZ7.1.H689 Big 2019 (print) | DDC [E]—dc23

Book design by Nicole Gastonguay

MANUFACTURED IN CHINA
10 9 8 7 6 5 4 3 2 1
First Edition

Random House Children's Books supports the First Amendment
and celebrates the right to read.

BIG BOYS CRY

JONTY HOWLEY

WITHDRAWN

RANDOM HOUSE
NEW YORK

IT WAS LEVI'S FIRST DAY AT A
NEW SCHOOL, AND LEVI WAS SCARED.

PAPA DIDN'T KNOW WHAT TO DO.

SO HE TOLD LEVI, "BIG BOYS DON'T CRY."

SO LEVI DIDN'T.

SCHOOL

ON HIS WAY, LEVI SAW A FISHERMAN WITH TEARS IN HIS EYES, SETTING OFF ON A LONG TRIP.

"BIG BOYS DON'T CRY," SAID LEVI.

NEXT, LEVI SAW A HARPIST,
LOST IN HIS MUSIC AND MEMORIES . . .

... AND SOME PASSIONATE POETS, PRACTICING THEIR PROSE.

"BIG BOYS *DON'T* CRY," WHISPERED LEVI.

NEW PARENTS,

LEVI SAW GRANDPARENTS,

SCHOOL

RICH MEN, AND NOT-SO-RICH MEN.

HE SAW PROUD MEN

ARMY MEN

YOUNG MEN

OLD MEN

BIKER MEN

BRAINY MEN

AND EVEN BAKER MEN CRYING!

IN FACT . . .

. . . BIG BOYS WERE

SOON ENOUGH, LEVI ARRIVED AT SCHOOL.

IN THE END, LEVI'S FIRST DAY WASN'T SO SCARY . . .

AND BEFORE HE KNEW IT,

IT WAS TIME TO GO HOME.

ON HIS WAY BACK, HE THOUGHT
ABOUT ALL HE'D SEEN.

WHEN LEVI GOT HOME, PAPA HAD TEARS IN HIS EYES.

"WHY ARE YOU CRYING?" ASKED LEVI.

"IT WAS YOUR FIRST DAY AT A NEW SCHOOL,"
SAID PAPA. "AND I WAS SCARED."

"PAPA . . . BIG BOYS DO CRY," SAID LEVI.

"AND THAT'S OKAY," SAID PAPA.

31901065032957